Barbie™
A Dancer's Dream

FUN WORKS

It was the last day of the ballet tryouts. Barbie was a finalist. She held her breath as the teacher read the list of dancers who would be part of the dance company. "We are only adding two new ballerinas this year, Jessica and . . . Barbie."

Barbie ran home to tell Skipper the good news. "I'm so excited," Barbie said hugging Skipper. "And I will be teaching a ballet class on Saturday mornings that you can take!" Skipper was so proud of her older sister. Barbie was a real ballerina now.

When Saturday morning came, Barbie and Skipper drove to the dance studio. There were five girls waiting outside. Barbie introduced herself and Skipper.

"Dancing has shown me that if I put my mind to it and work really hard, I can be something I've always wanted to be," Barbie explained.

Barbie watched the girls practicing the exercises she had given them—particularly a graceful girl named Tina. She was a good dancer, but she looked so unhappy.

Suddenly, Tina collapsed on the floor and began to cry. "Oooh, I told my mother I can't do this anymore."

Barbie put her arm around Tina's shoulders and took her outside. "Tina, you don't have to dance," Barbie told her. "But you're not really troubled about ballet, are you?"

"I used to love to dance," admitted Tina shyly. "But I was in a car accident, and ever since then I feel really scared. I just don't believe in myself anymore." Barbie gave Tina a hug and suggested she just watch for a while.

Week after week, Tina came to class and watched the other girls do their exercises. Finally they put some steps to music. "Let the music guide you," called Barbie. Tina closed her eyes and took a deep breath. One by one the other girls stopped dancing and stood to the side of the room. Tina was alone on the floor, dancing like a dream.

Nobody moved. As the music ended, Tina opened her eyes. Barbie applauded. Skipper and the girls ran up to Tina and hugged her.

For the first time in a long time, Tina felt happy to be dancing again.

After class, Barbie took the girls out for ice-cream sundaes. "I think we're ready to perform in public!" Barbie said excitedly.

"Even me?" Tina asked quietly. "Especially you," Barbie winked.

The day of the recital, the girls teased each other and laughed as they dressed in their beautiful ballet costumes and put on their makeup. Tina looked pale and never said a word. Barbie took her aside and held both her hands. "We are going to do this together," she promised.